For Hedwig and Ilse
~ Lisbeth Zwerger ~

Copyright © 2013 by NordSüd Verlag AG, CH-8005 Zürich, Switzerland.
First published in Germany under the title *Leonce und Lena.*
English translation copyright © 2013 by NorthSouth Books Inc., New York 10016.
English translation by David Henry Wilson.

First published in the United States, Great Britain, Canada, Australia, and New Zealand in 2013
by NorthSouth Books, Inc., an imprint of NordSüd Verlag AG, CH-8005 Zürich, Switzerland.

Distributed in the United States by NorthSouth Books Inc., New York 10016.
Library of Congress Cataloging-in-Publication Data is available.
ISBN: 978-0-7358-4141-3
Printed in Germany by Memminger MedienCentrum Druckerei
und Verlags-AG, Memmingen, October 2013.

1 3 5 7 9 · 10 8 6 4 2

www.northsouth.com

Georg Büchner

LEONCE AND LENA

A comedy

Illustrated by *Lisbeth Zwerger*

Retold by *Jürg Amann*

Characters:

King Peter of Popo
Prince Leonce, his son, engaged to:
Lena, Princess of Pipi
Valerio
Governess
Lord Chamberlain
Master of Ceremonies
President
Chaplain
Leader of the Council
Schoolmaster
Servants, councillors, peasants, etc.

A CONSERVATORY IN THE PALACE.

~

Leonce alone, draped over a bench.

LEONCE: Am I a loafing layabout? Do I have nothing to do? Oh yes, and it's so sad! Loafing around is the source of every vice. The things people do out of sheer boredom, though their faces are deadly serious while they do them. Why must I be the only one who realizes it? Why can't I take myself seriously and dress this poor old puppet up in coat and tails, and shove an umbrella in its hand so it'll look nice and honest and important and moral? Oh, if only we could just be someone else for a change!

A ROOM IN THE PALACE.

King Peter of Popo is being dressed by two valets.

KING PETER: Humans must think, but I must think for my subjects because they can't think for themselves. Where's my shirt, my trousers? Wait . . . ugh! Free will will be free. And where is morality? And where are my cuffs? Everything's all mixed up—two buttons too many buttoned up, and what's my snuffbox doing in my right-hand pocket? My whole system's ruined. Ha, what's this knot in my handkerchief for? What is the meaning of the knot? What, O knot, have I forgot? Ah. I know, I know. I wanted to remember my people. Gentlemen, come!

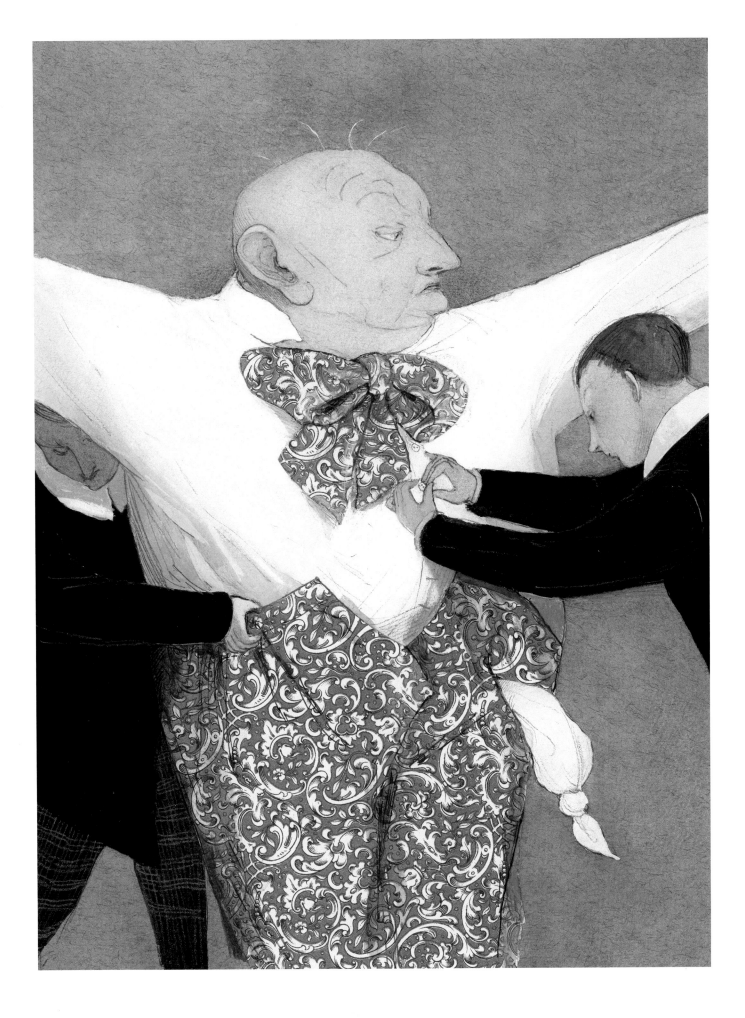

THE COUNCIL CHAMBER.

~

KING PETER: My very dear and faithful subjects, I wish hereby and herewith to tell you and inform you, and inform you and tell you that either my son will get married or he won't—either . . . or . . . You understand me, do you not? There is no third way.

A GARDEN.

Lena, Princess of Pipi, in her wedding finery, with the governess.

LENA: It's now. This is it. All this time I had nothing at all on my mind. Life simply passed by, and then suddenly I'm faced with this special day. And I've got a garland in my hair—and the bells, the bells! Oh God, I could certainly fall in love. Why not? You get so lonely, and you reach out for a hand to hold. But why does someone have to stick two hands together that weren't reaching out for each other? What's my poor little hand done to deserve this? The ring stings like an angry wasp.

GOVERNESS: But they say he's a knight in shining armor.

LENA: But a man . . .

GOVERNESS: Well?

LENA: . . . a man I don't love. A man I've never seen. Flowers open and close their petals when they feel like it to greet the morning sun or to escape from the evening wind. Is a king's daughter less free than a flower?

GOVERNESS: My poor child, my poor, dear child! I can't bear to see you like this. Perhaps, who knows? I might have an idea. We shall see.

OPEN COUNTRY.

~

Leonce and Valerio, who is carrying the suitcases.

VALERIO: By all the saints, Prince, the world is a mighty big building.

LEONCE: No it's not. It's not. It's like a narrow hall of mirrors—I daren't even stretch out a hand for fear I'll bump into something.

VALERIO: We've already crossed a dozen dukedoms, a fistful of fiefdoms, and a whole collection of kingdoms—all at breakneck speed in just half a day! And what for? Because you're supposed to become a king and marry a beautiful princess!

LEONCE: But Valerio, it's the ideal! I have in my mind's eye the ideal woman, and I must find her.

VALERIO: Confound it, now we're back at the border. This country's like an onion—one layer of skin after another; or a nest of boxes—in the biggest there's nothing but more boxes and in the smallest there's nothing at all.

OPEN COUNTRY.

~

Lena and the governess walking.

GOVERNESS: Someone's put a magic spell on the day. The sun's not setting, and it's ages since we ran away.

LENA: I'd like to go on and on like this. Day and night. Nothing stirs. There's a red glow of flowers over the fields, and the distant hills are lying on the earth like resting clouds.

GOVERNESS: But we've got to find shelter. It'll soon be night.

LENA: Yes, the flowers are closing their feathery petals to go to sleep, and the sunbeams are rocking the blades of grass like weary dragonflies.

A HILL. IN THE BACKGROUND IS AN INN.

~

Leonce and Valerio are in the garden outside the inn.
There is a panoramic view.

LEONCE: Oh Valerio, I'm so young, and the world is so old! What a strange evening! Down there everything's so still, and up above the clouds are moving and changing, and the sunshine comes and goes. The earth has rolled itself up like a frightened child.

OUTSIDE THE INN.

VALERIO: I don't know about you, but I'm getting a nice warm feeling. The sun looks to me like an inn sign, and the fiery clouds at the top look like an inscription: "Inn of the Golden Sun." The earth is like a table, and we're lying on it like playing cards: you are the king, I'm the jack, and all that's missing is a queen, a beautiful queen, with a nice big gingerbread heart on her breast. Good Lord, there she is!

ON THE PATH TO THE INN.

~

Lena and the governess appear.

VALERIO: Why, dear madam, do you hasten so fast that your legs are exposed right up to your garters?

GOVERNESS: Why, dear sir, do you open your mouth so wide that you create a gaping hole in the landscape?

VALERIO: So that you, dear madam, don't give yourself a bloody nose by bumping into the horizon.

ON THE PATH TO THE INN.

~

LENA (*to the governess*): Is the way so long?

LEONCE (*dreamily to himself*): Oh, every way is long. For tired feet every way is too long.

LENA (*who hears him*): And for tired eyes every light is too sharp, and for tired lips every breath is too heavy, and for tired ears every word is too much.

She and the governess enter the inn.

AT THE SIDE OF THE PATH TO THE INN.

LEONCE: Oh, that voice. "Is the way so long?" There are many voices on this earth that speak, and one might wonder what they're speaking about, but *her* I understood. "Is the way so long?"

A ROOM AT THE INN.

~

GOVERNESS: Stop thinking about that man!

LENA: He was so old beneath those blond curls. Spring on his cheeks and winter in his heart! It's so sad.

GOVERNESS: Where are you going, child?

LENA: I want to go down into the garden. You know, I should really have been put in a pot. I need dew and night air, like flowers. I can't stay in this room. The walls are crushing me.

THE MOONLIT GARDEN OUTSIDE THE INN.

VALERIO (*lying on the lawn*): It's lovely to be out in nature, but it would be even lovelier if there weren't any midges and if the hotel beds were a bit cleaner. There are people snoring inside and frogs croaking outside; crickets chirping inside and grasshoppers chirruping outside. Good night, dear lawn.

IN THE GRASS, NIGHT, MOONLIGHT.

~

LENA (*some distance away, talking to herself*): The warbler chirruped as she dreamed. The night sleeps on, her cheeks grow paler, her breath grows softer. The moon is like a sleeping child, and in her sleep her golden curls fall across her sweet face.

IN THE GRASS, MOONLIGHT.

Leonce appears.

LEONCE: O night, as balmy as the first that ever fell on Paradise.

LENA: Who's there?

LEONCE: A dream.

LENA: Dreams are blessed.

LEONCE: So dream yourself to blessings, and let me be your blessed dream.

LENA: No, leave me alone!

She jumps up and quickly exits.

BY THE RIVER, NIGHT, MOONLIGHT.

❧

LEONCE: It's all too much, too much! The whole of my existence is this *one* moment. More there cannot be. The earth is a bowl of dark gold. The light foams up in it and floods over the brim, turning into the shining pearls of stars. This one drop of bliss makes me into a precious vessel. Down, down, you sacred chalice!

He is about to jump into the river.

VALERIO: Stop, O highest of Highnesses!

LEONCE: Leave me alone!

VALERIO: I shall be relieved to leave you if you promise to leave here alive.

LEONCE: Idiot!

IN THE GRASS ON THE RIVERBANK, STILL NIGHT, STILL MOONLIGHT.

~

LEONCE: Confound it, you've robbed me of the most beautiful suicide one could ever imagine! Never in my life shall I find a more fitting moment, and the weather's absolutely perfect for it. But now I don't feel like it anymore.

THEY ARE WALKING. IT IS DAYBREAK.

VALERIO: Marry her? Does she even know who you are?

LEONCE: She knows only that she loves me.

VALERIO: And does Your Highness know who she is?

LEONCE: Idiot! Ask the carnation, ask the dewdrop their names.

VALERIO: Hm! Prince, will you make me prime minister if I unite you today, in your father's presence, with this indescribable and nameless lady? Will you give me your word?

LEONCE: I give you my word!

PALACE SQUARE.

~

The schoolmaster. The council leader. Peasants in their
Sunday best, holding branches of fir.

SCHOOLMASTER: Be bold, good people! Hold your branches out in front
of you, so that you will seem like a forest of fir trees, and your noses will
be like strawberries. And listen carefully: those at the back must keep
running ahead of those at the front, so it'll seem like there's twice as many
of you.

COUNCIL LEADER: Listen, all of you; it says in the program: "All subjects
shall of their own free will be dressed in their best clothes, look well fed,
and with happy faces line the main road." So don't let us down!

SCHOOLMASTER: Try to look respectable! Don't scratch behind your ears
or pick your noses when the royal couple pass by, and show them the right
emotions. You remember what I taught you? Eh? *Vi!*

PEASANTS: *Vi!*   SCHOOLMASTER: *Vat!*   PEASANTS: *Vat!*

SCHOOLMASTER: *Vivat!* You see, Councillor, how intelligence grows. Do
you realize they're speaking Latin?!

STATEROOM IN THE PALACE.

~

Lords and ladies in all their finery.

MASTER OF CEREMONIES: It's a total fiasco! Everything's ruined. The roast beef's burned to a cinder, congratulations are turning to sympathy, and the stiff collars are drooping like pigs' ears. The peasants' beards and fingernails are growing again, and the soldiers' hair is standing on end. To the windows, everybody! His Majesty's coming!

THE PALACE STATEROOM.

~

King Peter and the president enter.

KING PETER: So the princess has also disappeared. And there's still no trace of our beloved crown prince? Have my orders been obeyed? Are there people watching all the borders?

MC: Yes, Your Majesty. The view from this room allows us to keep watch over everything everywhere.

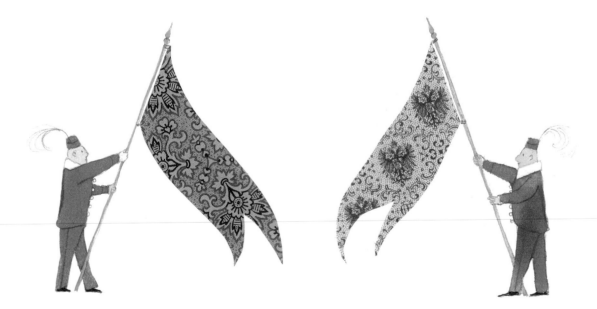

STILL THE STATEROOM.

MC: What have you seen?

1st SERVANT: A dog has been all over the kingdom looking for his master.

MC: And you?

2nd SERVANT: Someone's walking along the northern border—but it isn't the prince.

MC: And you?

3rd SERVANT: Sorry—nothing.

MC: That's not much. And you?

4th SERVANT: The same.

IN THE STATEROOM.

⁓

KING PETER: But did I not issue a decree that on this day my Royal Majesty was to enjoy himself, and that on this day there was to be a royal wedding?

PRESIDENT: Yes, Your Majesty, that's what was decreed and recorded in the minutes.

KING PETER: Did I not give my royal word? Very well, I shall now enforce my decree immediately and enjoy myself. Oh, I am so extraordinarily happy!

PRESIDENT: All of us share your feelings, Your Majesty, in so far as it is possible and seemly for us subjects to do so.

KING PETER: Oh, I don't know where to put myself, I'm so gloriously happy!

THE STATEROOM.

❧

KING PETER: But what about the wedding? Wasn't the other half of the decree that we should celebrate the wedding?

PRESIDENT: Yes, Your Majesty.

KING PETER: Yes. But if the prince doesn't come, and the princess doesn't come either?

PRESIDENT: Well, if the prince doesn't come, and the princess doesn't come either, then . . . then . . .

KING PETER: Then . . . then?

PRESIDENT: Then they won't be able to get married.

KING PETER: Stop! Is that a logical conclusion? If . . . then . . . Correct! But it was my command, my royal command!

THE STATEROOM, LATER.

⌒

KING PETER: You still can't see anything?

SERVANTS: Nothing. Nothing at all.

KING PETER: And I had decreed that I was to enjoy myself so, so much! I was going to start when the clock struck twelve, and I was going to enjoy myself for a full twelve hours. I'm beginning to feel quite melancholy.

PRESIDENT: All subjects are required to share the feelings of Your Majesty.

MC: Those who did not bring handkerchiefs with them are nevertheless, for decency's sake, forbidden to cry.

THE STATEROOM, A LITTLE LATER.

SERVANT: Hold on, I can see something! It's a sort of projection, a bit like a nose—the rest of it hasn't crossed the border yet . . . but now I see a man, and then two other people of different sexes.

MC: In what direction are they heading?

SERVANT: They're coming toward us. They're coming toward the palace.

THE STATEROOM, A LITTLE LATER STILL.

~

Valerio, Leonce, the governess, and Lena enter, all wearing masks.

SERVANT: Here they are!

KING PETER: Who are you?

VALERIO: Do I know? Am I this? Am I that? Or this and that? I could peel myself apart and . . . leaf through every layer.

KING PETER: But . . . but you must be something!

VALERIO: If Your Majesty so commands.

KING PETER: This fellow's getting me all confused. I am totally muddled and befuddled.

THE STATEROOM, IMMEDIATELY AFTERWARD.

～

VALERIO: What I actually wished to announce to this great and noble assembly is the fact that here before you are two world-famous automatons. You see here, ladies and gentlemen, two persons, one of each sex—one a man, one a woman—a gentleman and a lady. Nothing but art and engineering, nothing but a cardboard cover and clockwork springs. Each of them has a delicate ruby spring under the nail of the little toe of the right foot. You just have to touch it, and the mechanism will run for a good fifty years. They're very upper class, as you'll hear from their accents. But pay close attention, ladies and gentlemen, because they're just at a very interesting stage: the mechanism of love is beginning to express itself. The male has carried the female's shawl on a few occasions, and the female has fluttered her eyelids several times and looked up to heaven. And both of them have frequently whispered the words *faith*, *love*, and *hope*. They already appear to be in complete agreement about everything, and all that is missing is one little word: *amen*.

großer Karton
abspielte und
ihren Humor
worden ist,
bemüht sich
Umstand, daß
durchaus nicht
des Patien
und indem
Dr. Palócz
den schwersten
und Hautkra
die Behandlung
werde.

THE STATEROOM, IMMEDIATELY AFTERWARD.

KING PETER: In effigy? In effigy? Metaphorically, in their absence. President, if you hang someone in effigy, isn't that just as good as hanging them in person?

PRESIDENT: It's much better, because they don't have to suffer and yet they're hanged all the same.

KING PETER: That's it then! We'll celebrate the wedding in effigy! (*Indicating Leonce and Lena*) We'll pretend she's the princess and he's the prince. Let the bells ring!

THE PALACE CHAPEL.

⁓

CHAPLAIN: If Your Highness Leonce, Prince of Popo, and if Your Highness Lena, Princess of Pipi, and each of Your Highnesses mutually and reciprocally agree to have each other, then say loud and clear, "Yes."

LENA and LEONCE: Yes.

CHAPLAIN: Then I say amen.

THE PALACE COURTYARD, OUTSIDE THE CHAPEL.

~

VALERIO: Nicely done, short and sweet. So now you are man and wife. You can take off your masks.

ALL: The prince!

KING PETER: The prince, my son! I've been deceived! And who is this person?

GOVERNESS: The princess!

LEONCE: Lena?

LENA: Leonce?

LEONCE: Hey, Lena, I think that was an escape to Paradise.

THE PALACE COURTYARD, A LITTLE LATER.

LENA: O Coincidence!

LEONCE: O Providence!

THE PALACE COURTYARD, NOT MUCH LATER.

KING PETER: My children, I am moved, so moved I scarcely know what to say or do. I am the happiest man in the world. I hereby most solemnly place the crown in your hands, my son, and will at once, undisturbed, begin to think. Come, gentlemen, we must think; undisturbed, we must think.

Exit with the president.

THE PALACE GARDEN.

~

LEONCE: Well, Lena, what shall we do now? Ah, I know what you want to do. We'll have all clocks smashed, all calendars banned; and we shall count the hours and the moons solely according to the clock of the flowers, just by blossoms and by fruits.

LENA: Then we'll surround our little country with mirrors to catch the sun, so there will be no more winters; and in summer we'll take ourselves off to Ischia and Capri, and spend the whole year among roses and violets, oranges and laurels.

VALERIO: And I shall be prime minister and will issue a decree that anyone who works his fingers to the bone will be taken to court, and anyone who boasts of earning a living by the sweat of his brow will be declared insane and a danger to human society.

LEONCE AND LENA—A COMEDY OF PROTEST

"The whole of my existence is this *one* moment. More there cannot be." These words are spoken by Leonce after his first encounter with Lena, though he doesn't know who she is. Two people who were meant to be together have come together, even though—and indeed while—they are actually trying to escape from each other.

On the surface it would seem that Georg Büchner is following the Shakespearian tradition of the comedy of mistaken identities. However, in Büchner's play the identity problem goes a step further, because its central theme is dissatisfaction with the self and its restrictions. This is apparent at all times, even at the very beginning, when Leonce sighs: "Oh, if only we could just be someone else for a change!"

We are confronted here with a modern form of alienation. In a virtuoso display of finely tuned irony, Büchner is protesting against preconditioned and restrictive concepts of both individual and social life.

GEORG BÜCHNER was born in 1813 near Darmstadt, Germany. He has a very special place in the history of German literature. He was far in advance of his own time, and the subtle originality of his language and characterization makes him a forerunner of the modern theater.

He wrote the comedy *Leonce and Lena* for a literary competition but missed the deadline, and so the manuscript was returned to him unread. As a consequence of his revolutionary activities, he was forced to flee from the Hessian police and ended up in Zürich. There, at the age of twenty-three, he was awarded a doctorate but died shortly afterward of typhoid fever. His grave is on the Germaniahügel, part of the Zürichberg overlooking Zürich.

LISBETH ZWERGER was born in 1954 in Vienna, Austria, and studied there at the Academy of Art. She is internationally famous as an illustrator of classic fairy tales and has also provided brilliant illustrations for many works from world literature.

From early childhood she knew exactly what she wanted to do: illustrate children's books. Her very first publication, *Das fremde Kind* [*The Strange Child*] (1977), already showed her individual style and her ability to translate a text into vivid images. She also puts a gentle but nonetheless highly effective touch of humor into her characterizations, and clearly takes great pleasure in magic and mystery. All these qualities enable her pictures to enhance the attractions of a story without ever explaining it or giving away its secrets.

Concerning her work on *Leonce and Lena*, Lisbeth Zwerger says: "I have tried to 'translate' the playful and sometimes even flowery language into pictures with equally playful techniques, especially collage."

She has been awarded the Hans Christian Andersen Medal for her life's work.

JÜRG AMANN was born in 1947 in Winterthur, Switzerland. He began his career as a literary critic and dramaturge at the Schauspielhaus in Zürich, but in 1976 became a full-time writer. He won many prizes, including the highly prestigious Ingeborg-Bachmann-Preis, for his prose, plays, poetry, and essays. Over forty years, Jürg Amann produced a great deal of outstanding work. He died in 2013 at the age of sixty-five.

He was a passionate storyteller, a language artist, and a literary artisan in so far as he could take existing works in hand and with great sensitivity give them new life without changing their original character.

Jürg Amann had a lifelong fascination with Georg Büchner's plays. His very first book for NordSüd was a reworking of *Das Märchen von der Welt* [*The Tale of the World*] from Büchner's *Woyzeck*, enriching it with new poetic images and so creating a fresh reading experience.

In order to make *Leonce and Lena* accessible to young readers, he divided the text into short but vivid scenes. Wherever possible, he cut out the metaphysical profundities and the sharp cynicism while preserving the charm and insights of this poetically romantic love story.

The following is a selection of books
by Jürg Amann and/or Lisbeth Zwerger
available from NorthSouth Books:

The Fairy Tale of the World Büchner | Amann | Bhend

Ten Birds Amann | Gebert

The Wizard of Oz Baum | Zwerger

The Nutcracker Hoffmann | Zwerger

Thumbeline Andersen | Zwerger

Aesop's Fables Aesop | Zwerger

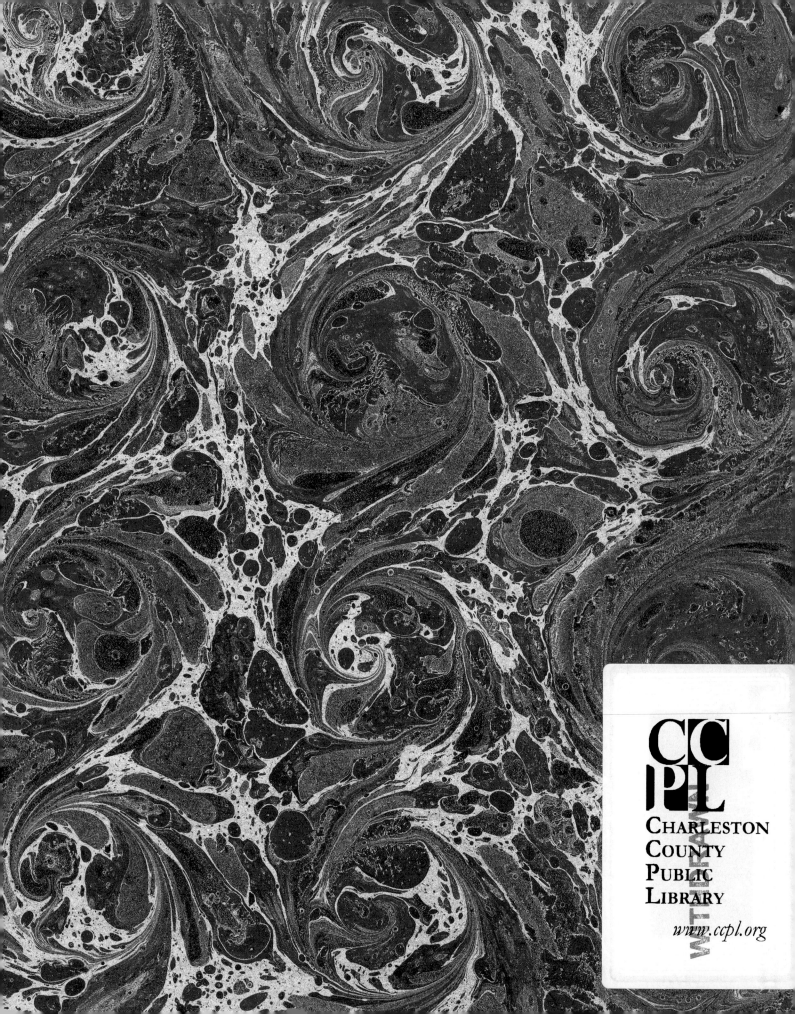